Rock Video's Megastars . . .

Phil Collins
Whitney Houston
Heart
Sade
John Cougar Mellencamp
Howard Jones
Belinda Carlisle
El DeBarge
U2
Huey Lewis and the News
Mr. Mister
Janet Jackson
Tears For Fears
Peter Gabriel
a-ha
The Monkees

. . . And more! Take an inside look at your favorite rock video stars. Get the most up-to-the-minute information about their latest videos. Read this photo-filled sequel to *ROCK VIDEO SUPERSTARS* and discover who's hot on the rock video scene.

Pleasant Valley School
DISTRICT 62
4623 West Redbud Drive
Peoria, Illinois 61604

Books by Daniel Cohen

GHOSTLY TERRORS
THE GREATEST MONSTERS IN THE WORLD
HORROR IN THE MOVIES
THE MONSTERS OF STAR TREK
MONSTERS YOU NEVER HEARD OF
REAL GHOSTS
SCIENCE FICTION'S GREATEST MONSTERS
STRANGE AND AMAZING FACTS ABOUT
  STAR TREK
SUPERMONSTERS
THE WORLD'S MOST FAMOUS GHOSTS

Books by Daniel and Susan Cohen

HEROES OF THE CHALLENGER
THE KID'S GUIDE TO HOME COMPUTERS
ROCK VIDEO SUPERSTARS
ROCK VIDEO SUPERSTARS II
WRESTLING SUPERSTARS
WRESTLING SUPERSTARS II

Available from ARCHWAY paperbacks

Most Archway Paperbacks are available at special quantity discounts for bulk purchases for sales promotions, premiums or fund raising. Special books or book excerpts can also be created to fit specific needs.

For details write the office of the Vice President of Special Markets, Pocket Books, 1230 Avenue of the Americas, New York, New York 10020.

ROCK VIDEO SUPERSTARS II

DANIEL AND SUSAN COHEN

AN ARCHWAY PAPERBACK
Published by POCKET BOOKS • NEW YORK

Cover photograph of Nancy Wilson © 1986 Dave Plastik/Retna Ltd. Cover photograph of Phil Collins © 1985 Scott Weiner/Retna Ltd. Cover photograph of Whitney Houston © 1986 Van Der Vooren/Retna Ltd. Cover photograph of John Cougar Mellencamp © 1985 Harrison Funk/Retna Ltd.

AN ARCHWAY PAPERBACK *Original*

An Archway Paperback published by
POCKET BOOKS, a division of Simon & Schuster, Inc.
1230 Avenue of the Americas, New York, N.Y. 10020

Copyright © 1987 by Daniel and Susan Cohen

All rights reserved, including the right to reproduce
this book or portions thereof in any form whatsoever.
For information address Pocket Books, 1230 Avenue
of the Americas, New York, N.Y. 10020

ISBN: 0-671-63397-X

First Archway Paperback printing January 1987

10 9 8 7 6 5 4 3 2 1

AN ARCHWAY PAPERBACK and colophon are
registered trademarks of Simon & Schuster, Inc.

Printed in the U.S.A.

IL 4+

Acknowledgments

Many people helped us with this book and we wish we could thank all of them. The authors would like to extend a special thank you to the following people for giving us special assistance. Tom Cording, Elektra/Asylum; Vicky Rose, The Howard Bloom Organization; Trudy Green, Front Line Management; Tom Hulett, Concerts West; Jeb Stuart-Bullock, E.S.P. Management; Ken Valdiserris, The Chicago Bears; Judy Hutson, Tin Pan Apple; Mary Klauzer, Lookout Management; Ed Bicknell, Damage Management; Gail Colson and Norma Bishop, Gailforce Management; Cary Baker, I.R.S. Records; Veronica Brice, DeMann Entertainment; Jonathon Lieberman and Mary Jo Mysezelow, RCA Records; Joanne Browne, A&M Records; Jim Slyman, The Howard Bloom Organization; Lisa Silfen, MTV; Paul King, Outlaw Management.

Contents

Rock Video Makes History / 1
Phil Collins / 8
Whitney Houston / 13
Heart / 18
Sade / 23
John Cougar Mellencamp / 25
Howard Jones / 31
Belinda Carlisle / 36
Simply Red / 40
El DeBarge / 44
Simple Minds / 49
U2 / 53
Tom Petty and the Heartbreakers / 58
Huey Lewis and the News / 62
Mr. Mister / 67
Janet Jackson / 71

Tears For Fears / 75
The Moody Blues / 78
Peter Gabriel / 83
The Fat Boys / 87
a-ha / 90
Dire Straits / 94
Jackson Browne / 98
The Monkees / 103
George Michael / 107
Films, Comics, and Musclemen / 110

ROCK VIDEO SUPERSTARS II

ROCK VIDEO MAKES HISTORY

On Saturday, July 13, 1985, a televised rock concert made history. It was seen by more people than any other live television event—ever. An estimated one and a half billion—that's *billion*—people worldwide watched this concert. Compare that to the mere 685 million who watched the first moon landing.

This rock concert originated in several different locations. The main events were held in London and Philadelphia. But there were live broadcasts from other places, including some Russian rock straight from Moscow. The concert was beamed off nine satellites to 100 different countries. And it went off practically without a hitch. It was a technical marvel. In the U.S., the concert was broadcast by the 24-hour music video channel, MTV.

Bob Geldof
(John Bellissimo)

You were probably one of those who watched part of this historic event. It's something you'll remember all of your life.

Of course this wasn't an ordinary concert. It was a concert called Live Aid. The aim was to raise money for the starving people in Africa. Millions of dollars were raised.

The man who inspired and organized the whole concert was a thirty-three-year-old Irish singer named Bob Geldof. Geldof was no newcomer to raising money through rock. In 1984 he saw a television report on the famine in the African country of Ethiopia. He was horrified. Geldof decided to do something to help the starving people. He got some of his friends and fellow musicians together to make a record and a video. The money from the project was to be used for the cause of African relief.

Some of the biggest names in British rock—David Bowie, Phil Collins, Wham!, Duran Duran, Culture Club—donated their time. The project was called Band Aid. The record the group made, "Do They Know It's Christmas?," became the fastest selling single in Britain and the U.S.

Geldof's success with Band Aid inspired a lot of other aid projects. The big one in America was USA for Africa. Forty-five top artists, including Bruce Springsteen, Cyndi Lauper, Madonna, and Huey Louis, just to name a few, got together to sing "We Are The World," a song written by Michael Jackson and Lionel Richie. Sales of that record broke records. The video made at the recording session was the most popular video ever, as well as one of the most moving.

Then came the big Live Aid concert. And it didn't stop there. Benefits were sponsored for a variety of causes. There was a tour and concert for Amnesty International, the organization that helps political prisoners throughout the world. Farm Aid, organized by country singer Willy Nelson, raised money for hard-pressed farmers in the U.S. Hands Across

Peter Gabriel at the Amnesty International Concert
(© 1986 Barry Morgenstein/MWA)

Eric Bazilian of the Hooters at the Amnesty International Concert
(John Bellissimo)

America, a project to raise money for the hungry and homeless in the U.S., wasn't a concert, but it had been inspired by Live Aid. That project was organized by rock star manager Ken Kragen. There was an anti-apartheid record and video. Other entertainers did their part. Comedians staged Comic Relief for the homeless. Even the heavy metal musicians, who pride themselves on being irresponsible, got together to do Hear'N Aid to raise money for Africa.

The fans have been very generous and have donated a lot of money, but the problems have not been solved. People are still starving in Africa. There are still homeless and hungry in the United States. Farmers are still losing their farms. People are still in prison because of what they believe. Bob Geldof never thought all the world's problems could be solved easily. Raising money was only part of what these events were meant to accomplish. What Geldof also wanted to do was to get people concerned and involved. He said he wanted to make it "fashionable to care." He has certainly done that.

When we were putting this book together, we were struck by how many stars were deeply involved, and did care. Not only did they appear at the various events, they were writing and singing songs about how we should all care more about other people.

Geldof has said that rock music "can become incredibly important when it is used as a huge moral force for good." In the last year or so that seems to have been happening. Sure, rock is basically entertainment. It's fun. And that's what it should be. But if you listen carefully to what some of the musicians have been saying, you'll realize it can be more.

Kenny Loggins at the Amnesty International Concert
(John Bellissimo)

PHIL COLLINS

Phil Collins isn't young. He isn't good-looking. He wears ordinary clothes. But when it comes time for him to perform, watch out! He's pure charisma. Cool and relaxed, he doesn't need outrageous costumes or elaborate special effects to make his own personal statement. Nobody around generates more excitement or star quality than Phil. It's hardly surprising then that so many people of all ages, from kids to senior citizens, think he's great. Credit part of his skill as a performer to his innate acting talent. Phil started his life in show biz as an actor.

At the age of fourteen, he played the role of the Artful Dodger in a London production of the Lionel Bart musical *Oliver*. (You may have seen the movie version of *Oliver*, which shows

Phil Collins

up regularly on television.) Though Phil enjoyed acting, he liked music even better.

Born in Chiswick, England in 1951, Phil was given a toy drum at the age of five and by the age of twelve was playing real drums. Never one to wait, Phil was already part of a well-received combo called Flaming Youth when he was only seventeen, an age when most future musicians are still only dreaming about a professional career. Flaming Youth lasted long enough to put out a record called *Ark 2*, which was chosen best album of the month by a major British music publication.

After Flaming Youth broke up, Phil heard that a band named Genesis was looking for a drummer. So he auditioned and was hired. Genesis was by no means an unknown band at that time. The group was about to cut its third album. But it was not the fabulously successful band it is today. It would take time, hard work, and the great gifts of Phil Collins to put Genesis at the very top.

Peter Gabriel, who has plenty of talent in his own right, was the lead singer of Genesis when Phil joined the band. But in 1975 Peter left the band to strike out on his own. People in the know assumed that Peter's going would mean the end of Genesis. To everyone's amazement, however, drummer Phil Collins stepped forward to take Peter Gabriel's place as the group's main vocalist. But could he sing? The question has been answered with a resounding "yes."

Genesis remained Phil's home base, but he was versatile enough to reach out in other directions, too. He began doing session work with many noted bands and artists. In 1975 he joined a jazz-fusion ensemble called Brand X, staying with the group for seven years. Phil recorded seven albums with Brand X, but that didn't stop him from recording and touring with Genesis. If there's one thing Phil Collins has plenty of, it's energy.

Phil Collins and Marilyn Martin

As if all this weren't enough, Phil made a solo album, *Face Value,* in 1981 and followed it up with a second solo album, *Hello, I Must Be Going!,* a year later. Both albums spawned hit singles and brought audiences out in force for Phil's first solo tour. Next, Phil turned to producing albums for artists like Adam Ant, Philip Bailey, and Eric Clapton. Phil's song "Easy Lover," which he performed with Philip Bailey, was not only a major hit single, but also a smashingly good and highly popular video.

Phil played drums on Robert Plant's first two solo albums and toured the U.S. with him. Phil was one of the rock singers you heard on the Band Aid recording of "Do They Know It's Christmas?," which raised money for the people starving in famine-stricken Ethiopia. The ever-busy Phil Collins wrote and recorded the title song for the movie *Against All Odds*, which earned him his first number-one, top-of-the-chart record in the United States. His extraordinarily successful album, *No Jacket Required*, is aptly titled. Phil is distinctly not a jacket and tie type. Ease and informality suit him best.

What could Phil Collins do to top his already enormous list of musical achievements? Well, he might launch an acting career. After all, he's already appeared on the popular television series, *Miami Vice*. On the other hand, he could just go right on being one of the world's best musical entertainers, writing songs, recording them, and making stellar videos. He's one classy guy, Phil Collins.

To contact Phil Collins write:

Atlantic Records
75 Rockefeller Plaza
New York, NY 10020

WHITNEY HOUSTON

When Clive Davis, president of Arista records, was introducing Whitney Houston on the Merv Griffin show, he said, "You either got it or you don't. She's got it." He might have said, "She's got it all."

Let's start with looks. Whitney has been a professional model, with magazine covers and photo spreads in such publications as *Glamour, Seventeen, Young Miss,* and *Cosmopolitan.* Whitney describes her modeling image as "young, kind of innocent, but sexy."

Then there is her family background. Her mother is the legendary gospel and soul singer, Cissy Houston, who, as founder and leader of The Sweet Inspirations, has sung with such musical greats as Aretha Franklin and Elvis Presley. The famous Dionne Warwick is Whitney's first cousin.

Whitney Houston
(© 1986 Andrea Laubach/Retna Ltd.)

With such a family, it's natural that Whitney got off to an early start singing. She began singing gospel in the choir of the New Hope Baptist Church in Newark, New Jersey where her mother is the minister of music. By the age of fifteen, Whitney was singing in Cissy Houston's nightclub act, at first doing background vocals, but then eventually sharing the spotlight with her mother. One critic who saw the show in 1982 wrote, "Eighteen-year-old Whitney solos on two numbers, and has the looks, voice, and style of Lena Horne when she was that age. Star material."

Over the next few years, Whitney began appearing as a background vocalist on many albums, including records by Lou Rawls, Chaka Khan, The Neville Brothers, Paul Jabara, and Material.

So Whitney Houston seemed destined for stardom, though few would have predicted how quickly her stardom would come. Her debut album rapidly became the best-selling album by a black female vocalist in pop music history. The numbers are staggering. The album spent more than sixty weeks on *Billboard's* Pop Album charts, with nine weeks at number one. Sales are currently over ten million worldwide. The album has also yielded four top-ten singles, three of which have reached number one on *Billboard's* pop singles chart.

Whitney has also headlined sold-out concerts at Carnegie Hall, appeared with Jermaine Jackson on the soap, *As the World Turns,* and been featured on a host of magazine covers. Her videos have topped MTV popularity charts. And just in case you missed her all of these other places, she was also featured in a national commercial for Diet Coke. All of this happened to Whitney Houston in 1986 when she was only twenty-two years old.

Now, there have been other success stories in the pop and rock world. Many of them have faded rapidly, so that the superstar of five years ago is barely remembered today. But Whitney's fame is based on solid talent.

The *New York Times,* far from a trendy music publication, said, ". . . Miss Houston's musical worth is already beyond question. An extraordinary singer whose flexible, rangy pop-gospel voice has a core of steel, she is the heir apparent to the female soul tradition of Aretha Franklin, Gladys Knight, and her first cousin Dionne Warwick. Artistically, her debut album is a personal triumph . . ."

The *Times* continued, "Of all the overnight sensations pop music has produced so far this decade, Whitney Houston stands the best chance of being as big a star ten years from now as she is today."

Whitney has handled her overwhelming success with a coolness and a professionalism which astonishes most people who meet her. "I've watched [my mother] and my cousin [Dionne Warwick] throughout the years, so I think I was a little better prepared for show business than someone just getting off the bus in New York City or something."

Most stars today have their private lives

spread all over the supermarket tabloids and the TV gossip shows. Not Whitney. She has a private life that is truly private. When asked about romance her reply is not very informative: "I'm really too busy for a relationship; I'm just not in one place long enough."

Though she travels a lot, Whitney still calls Newark home; she has an apartment not far from the neighborhood where she grew up and where her mother still lives.

To contact Whitney Houston write:

Arista Records Inc.
Arista Building
6 West 57th Street
New York, NY 10019

HEART

Heart has had rock journalists reaching for all the clichés about "Open Heart Surgery," "Heart Transplants," "Heart Still Beating," etc., etc. Heart was big in the late seventies, but went into a serious, nearly fatal decline in the early eighties. Now they're back, and bigger than ever. There have been comebacks before in rock—but not many as spectacular as that of Heart.

The heart of Heart are the sisters Nancy and Ann Wilson. They started out as two Beatle-obsessed teenagers in Seattle, Washington.

"We were both ugly ducklings—and still are, off and on," Nancy told *Rolling Stone* reporter Laura Fissinger. "Maybe that's one reason we had a chance to become people, know what I mean. We were always overweight or too thin,

Heart
(Greg Gorman, courtesy Front Line)

or sick or had braces, or we were too counter-culture, or studying too much. Or we were playing guitars instead of socializing."

"We were raised by a liberated woman to think that we could do whatever the heck we wanted," added Ann. ". . . there were just no limits on what girls could do."

Success in rock has always been tough for women. Ann had it relatively easy because she's the singer, one of the best in the business. Nancy, however, is a guitarist; women are not supposed to play headbanger guitar the way

Nancy does. From the start, however, the sisters have always stuck together.

The group began in Seattle, but soon followed their first manager and sound man to Vancouver, Canada where they gained their first success. Some of Heart's early tours included bizarre activities such as dodging moose in northern Alberta. But soon Canadians took to the group, and they won a Juno, a sort of Canadian Grammy, for Best Group of 1976. That was also the year they recorded their first album, *Dreamboat Annie*. A member of the band, guitarist Howard Leest, was working for Mushroom Records in Vancouver. First Mushroom wanted Anne as a solo act—remember females could sing but could not be instrumentalists. Heart held out, and finally Mushroom agreed to take the whole band. Much to everyone's delight, their first album was a huge hit.

Success also brought trouble. Heart tried to switch from Mushroom to a larger, better-known U.S. record company. The whole thing wound up in a very messy court battle. Even messier was the departure of manager Mike Fisher and his brother Roger, one of the group's guitarists. It was more than a professional move, as the Wilson sisters had been romantically involved with the Fisher brothers. "Our biggest mistake was allowing romance within the band. It's suicide," says Ann Wilson today. There were more personnel changes in 1982, and record sales were slumping badly as well.

"We were in the muck," says Ann, "and we had to pull ourselves out."

It was time to shake things up. And shake they did. They got new management and signed with a new label which they felt believed in them. They also got a new producer for their new album—Ron Nevison. Cutting a record with the strong-willed Nevison wasn't easy. "I hated every minute of it," Ann told the Canadian publication *Rock Express*, of the three-month recording session. But the product was the album *Heart*, the band's most successful album ever. The combination had clicked, and now Heart and Nevison are planning another album. "That won't be pleasant either," says Ann.

The new Heart videos display a bold and sexy look which has caused almost as much comment as the group's new sound. Actually, say the Wilson sisters, the look isn't that new, since they've always had it in their stage act. It's just new to the videos. The video fans seem to love it, and Heart videos have consistently appeared in the top 20 for 1986.

So, if we want to reach into the cliché bag—the beat of Heart is stronger than ever.

To contact Heart write:

Capitol Records, Inc.
1750 North Vine Street
Hollywood, CA 90028

SADE

If anyone has a corner on grace, sophistication, and elegance, it's Sade, whose debut album, *Diamond Life,* produced glittering sales figures. The record went gold within two months of its release, and not long after that it went platinum. Although she's basically a quiet person with simple tastes, Sade's glamorous but demure style makes audiences of kids feel grown up, and grown-up audiences feel young.

Sade was born Helen Folasade Adu in a village in Nigeria, fifty miles from the city of Lagos. The name Sade is an abbreviation of her African middle name Folasade. She is the daughter of an African father and English mother. Her parents separated when she was four years old and Sade moved with her

Sade
(© Ian McKeil/Retna Ltd.)

mother to London. By the time she was a teenager Sade was studying music, and working part-time in a variety of jobs, from bicycle messenger to waitress. She went on to study fashion design at St. Martin's College but gave up designing to sing in a jazz-funk band called Pride. The band fell apart, but Sade went on.

Early in 1984, CBS Records signed her to a contract and the ultra classy, ultra gorgeous Sade made *Diamond Life*. The rest is history.

To contact Sade write:

CBS Records (EPIC/Portrait)
1801 Century Park West
Los Angeles, CA 90067

JOHN COUGAR MELLENCAMP

Some rock stars lead the glitzy life when they become famous. They move to big cities, ride around in fancy cars, and wear expensive clothes. Not so John Cougar Mellencamp. He was born in the Midwest, in America's heartland, and that's where he still lives. He wears old clothes, rides around on a motorcycle, and doesn't think being a rock star makes him better than anyone else. In other words, he's very human, very real. And his music shows it.

John's hometown is Seymour, Indiana—near Bloomington, where the University of Indiana is located. Seymour isn't now, and wasn't then, a wealthy place. There wasn't much for a teenager to do there when John was growing up, except drive past the farms and maybe go to a dance once in a while. That's pretty much what John did. As for school, it didn't interest him, but fortunately music did. At fourteen he got a guitar, and at fifteen he began playing with a band called Crepe Sole. During his senior year of high school, he got married and after graduation became a broadcast journalism major at Indiana's Vincennes University. So far this could be the story of a lot of young guys with strong family ties, strong roots, and not many opportunities.

Though John loved Indiana, he also loved music, and it was this particular love that drove him to the biggest city in America, New York, when he was twenty-two, while his wife and young daughter, Michelle, remained in the Midwest. Then, what seemed like a magnificent stroke of luck occurred. John was "discovered" by a top show-biz agency and given a chance to make a record. It looked like the kind of big break every young performer dreams of, a ticket to the top.

Unfortunately, the big break turned out to be a big disappointment. Take John's name. You won't find Cougar on his birth certificate. To the publicity people in charge of John's career Johnny Cougar sounded kind of country, even wild. It didn't matter that John didn't like it. They called him Johnny Cougar anyway. Then there was the hype, the campaign to make John a star. John was back in Indiana by then, where the limos and the interviews with rock critics seemed phony. So he said good-bye to his agent and the record company and began slogging his way to the top the hard way.

He played clubs in and around Bloomington and eventually went to England. There he recorded an album for a new company called Riva Records. The album became popular in France, England, and Australia where John briefly hosted a rock 'n' roll television show. John received some recognition as a songwriter when Pat Benatar recorded his "I Need a Lover." In 1978, John and his band, Zone, got a real break, touring as the opening act for Kiss. He brought out his first American album in 1979.

John's career was changing. So was his personal life. In 1981, he and his first wife were divorced, and he married a woman from Los Angeles who soon got used to the slower pace of life in Indiana. They have a daughter, Teddy Jo. The next big event in John's life was when he went to Miami, to not only make a record, but to produce it. The record was *American Fool*. Helped along by some excellent videos, it became the top-selling album in America.

If there were any doubts that John's rural background was genuine, he dispelled them when he appeared on the "American Music Awards" in old blue jeans and a denim jacket.

John Cougar Mellencamp and winner of the MTV Party House Susan Miles of Bellvue, Washington
(Mark Weiss)

He went even further in establishing his rural image when he began cutting records in a farmhouse called the Shack, not far from the modest house he lives in.

Speaking of houses, one of John's best and most famous songs is called "Pink Houses." John isn't the kind of songwriter and musician who cares only about rhythm and sound. His songs come out of the experiences of real people and they have meaning. Sometimes they're sad songs. John has been influenced by Woody Guthrie, a folksinger who wrote about what many Americans went through in the era of the Depression, the 1930s. As the word Depression implies, it was a down time and great numbers of people were out of work and poor.

The video for "Pink Houses" was so effective and the song so popular that MTV and John's record company, Polygram, sponsored a contest in 1984—the grand prize was a pink house in Bloomington, Indiana. If you watch MTV, you know how much fun the contests are. The lucky winner of this one was Susan Miles of Seattle, Washington, who got to Bloomington in time for both a housewarming and a house-painting party.

John's ideals run deep. Unlike most superstars, he doesn't crave huge audiences, but prefers to play small halls, many of them in towns and cities off the beaten path, where rock stars rarely go. On his album, *Scarecrow,* he sang about the tragedy of American farmers losing their farms. But that wasn't enough for John. He helped organize Farm Aid to raise money to save family-run farms. You can be sure that from the stages of rock clubs or from the cornfields of Indiana, John Mellencamp will go right on being a true American troubador.

To contact John Cougar Mellencamp write:

Polygram Records
810 Seventh Avenue
New York, NY 10019

John Cougar Mellencamp Fan Club
P.O. Box 1785
Bloomington, Indiana 47402

HOWARD JONES

Howard Jones has been called a microchip minstrel and a high-tech hippie. Certainly, this likable young Englishman has emerged as one of the masters of the new music technology. He's widely admired by the experts. Philip Bashe, writing in the magazine *International Musician,* praises Jones's "impressive display of technical wizardry, much of which is no doubt lost on a sizable percentage of his audience."

Howard is more than a technician, or a "musician's musician." He has become an extremely popular performer as well. Though Howard says he's not out to preach sermons to anyone, there are some messages that come through very strongly in his music. Among

Howard Jones
(Simon Fowler, 1985; courtesy Elektra/Asylum)

them are optimism, the importance of carrying on in the face of setbacks, and the need to think for yourself rather than blindly accepting authority.

Certainly, the importance of carrying on in the face of setbacks is a message that could be drawn from Howard's own career. Sometimes, when a performer suddenly bursts on the scene, he seems like an overnight success. But Howard Jones was twenty-nine years old before he made his mark. And he had years of hardship behind him.

Howard was born in the relatively affluent region of High Wycombe, England. He was the eldest of four sons. The Jones family originally came from Wales, and the Welsh people have a strong musical tradition. The brothers often sang four-part harmonies.

Howard got his first piano when he was eight years old. Later, he attended the Royal Northern School of Music to study classical piano. He didn't like it. The school was too rigid for him. "All the things I was good at they didn't cater to," he said. "I was a misfit."

While in school, Howard was playing in bands—loads of them. He was incredibly hardworking and persistent, even when nothing seemed to be going right. "He was always very single-minded," says his brother Martin.

Howard Jones was also pretty sure that somehow he was going to make it. But he wasn't sure that it would be as a member of a band. "I'd been in a lot of bands," he says, "and there was always so much arguing nothing ever got done."

By 1980, Howard had discovered synthesizers. With the new electronic equipment he could, essentially, become a one man band. That's just what happened. As his skill with synthesizers grew so did his audience. "Once the ball got rolling," says Howard, "everywhere I played was packed. There was a core of followers that would even rent buses to travel up to London to see me play there."

But there still weren't any record contracts. And the club dates didn't pay that well. Howard was working days as a fruit and vegetable delivery driver with his wife Jan. "There were definitely times when I felt like giving up."

Of course, he didn't give up, and when his opportunity finally came he made the most of it. Ironically, it was Jan's injury in an auto accident that provided the opportunity. The Joneses used the settlement money from the accident to invest in a battery of synthesizers. These form the basis of Howard's music. They also got him his long-awaited record contract. Howard's first singles were instant hits in England.

His solo stage show, featuring an incredible array of electronic equipment, plays to packed houses. Recently Howard has added his brother Martin as bassist, drummer Trevor Moralis, and a backing vocal trio to the show. But there is never any doubt that Howard Jones is the boss, and that they are playing the music he created.

There are, however, other technical wizards in music today. Howard Jones's success is based as much on his soulful voice, and simple, heartfelt songs, as it is on his mastery of the keyboards and sequencers.

There is a strong moral side to many of Howard's songs. It is not surprising that he interrupted a very profitable North American tour so that he could appear at the Live Aid concert. "I think it's important to be true to your word. If I sing about the things I sing about then I should endeavor as much as possible to be that. I think that's my responsibility. If I didn't try to live up to the things I sing about it would take all of the weight out of it. I think that's the biggest responsibility."

Howard tries to bring big political and moral issues down to a personal level. "It's so much more glamorous and high profile to try to tackle international, global things. But I think that the real glory lies in people changing their own attitudes in their own lifetimes."

One thing that Howard has strong personal feelings about is cruelty to animals. He's a dedicated vegetarian, and says he's investigating the possibilities of starting a chain of vegetarian fast-food restaurants.

Howard Jones is very much his own man and in complete control of his career. Right now he's making the most of it.

To contact Howard Jones write:

Elektra Records
75 Rockefeller Plaza
New York, NY 10019

BELINDA CARLISLE

There's something summery about Belinda Carlisle, former lead singer of the Go-Go's, now a solo act out on her own. Maybe it's her blond hair and golden California good looks. Maybe it's because the Go-Go's songs were big car-radio hits, the kind of music you listened to while driving to the beach in July. Or maybe it's because one of the Go-Go's biggest triumphs came on a moonlit summer night when they had seventeen thousand fans dancing and cheering at the Hollywood Bowl in Los Angeles.

When the Go-Go's got their start in 1977, some people thought of them as just the latest "girl group." But really, they were an all-woman rock 'n' roll band. Right away that made them something special. Most rock 'n' roll bands are strictly male.

Belinda Carlisle
(Courtesy I.R.S. Records)

It was the band's 1982 debut album, *Beauty And The Beat*, that made them stars. For seven weeks the album was number one on *Billboard's* charts. The album went multi-platinum, and the Go-Go's two following albums produced the top ten hit singles "Vacation," "Head Over Heels," "Our Lips Are Sealed," and the smash hit, million-selling "We Got The Beat." The popular *Talk Show* was the Go-Go's third album.

Together for seven years, the Go-Go's crisscrossed America, their tour bus going from gig to gig, audiences growing as their fame spread. But nothing is forever, and in 1985 the members of the Go-Go's felt it was time to pursue separate careers. In the summer of 1986, Belinda Carlisle brought out her solo album, aptly titled *Belinda,* a collection of eleven songs. Charlotte Caffey, former lead guitarist for the Go-Go's, added her own special touch to the record, co-writing songs and providing background vocals and guitar parts.

Career changes are always both risky and exciting moments for stars. Belinda worked very hard preparing her new record, devoting all her energy to making her solo move a success. She studied with a vocal coach, taking lessons three times a week. She assembled her band with care. She rehearsed like crazy. She also went on a diet, emerging sleek and glamorous. Then, when she was convinced the time was right, she stepped into the recording studio.

To help launch her new career there was a two-night headline debut at the Roxy Theatre in Los Angeles. This was followed by a tour of cities in the United States and Canada. Of course, there was a video. Belinda chose to make a video of her first single, "Mad About You." Making good videos comes naturally to Belinda. After all, it was a video that first got the Go-Go's going. Up till that first video, the macho world of rock didn't take the Go-Go's seriously. "Mad About You" is a visually enchanting ode to the photogenic Belinda. If the romance on the video looks real, maybe it's because the man in the video is Belinda's husband. As for her bright smile and charm, that didn't need changing. Watching Belinda Carlisle on video is like waking up to a sunny day.

To contact Belinda Carlisle write:

I.R.S.
(International Record Syndicate, Inc.)
445 Park Avenue, 6th Floor
New York, NY 10022

SIMPLY RED

Mick Hucknall, organizer and lead singer of Simply Red, grew up in the depressed industrial city of Manchester in the north of England. But musically, he says, it was like growing up in America, listening to the records of James Brown and Aretha Franklin. A lot of kids from England's industrial north tried to adapt the sounds of American soul music. "We called it northern soul," says Hucknall.

"So what if I didn't sing in my father's church like Aretha Franklin? I'm from a working-class background. I don't think you can make any big deal of it being American music. It's the music that was there in my home town when I was a child. It was as if we were in the suburbs of Detroit, we heard it so much. It was as much our music."

The young British boy also listened to a lot

of the older jazz musicians such as Charlie Mingus and Miles Davis.

Hucknall recalls that he had his first "professional" singing engagement when he was just six years old. It was "at an auntie's wedding with an adult band behind me. I think I sang 'I Wanna Hold Your Hand.' "

It wasn't a clear road to success after that early start. In fact, there were lots of hard times, and second thoughts about music as a career. Hucknall deejayed at a club in Manchester while going to art school.

After that, he was involved for three years with a punk band with the wonderful name The Frantic Elevators. That band never made any money. "I was on the dole," says Hucknall.

Then, in early 1984, Hucknall got the idea for a new kind of band, one that used the rhythm and blues/jazz and soul influenced music that he had grown up with. The result was Simply Red. The name was probably inspired by Hucknall's brilliant copper-colored hair, which spirals out in long curls over his forehead and makes his video image memorable.

The band, which currently consists of Chris Joyce, Tim Kellert, Sylvan Richardson, Fritz McIntyre, Tony Bowers, and Hucknall, began making itself known in England in 1985, and by mid-1986 had become known to American audiences as well.

Simply Red
(Courtesy Elektra/Asylum)

Simply Red

What really helped the band's success in America is its striking and moving video for "Holding Back the Years," Hucknall's account of hard times among the many unemployed in northern England. By mid 1986, "Holding Back the Years" was topping the charts in the U.S.

Hucknall is more than willing to discuss politics, but he views his band as strictly commercial: "I see it as pop music more than anything else—pop music that's got a little more taste." However, one can't watch the video for "Holding Back the Years" without feeling that Simply Red is looking for something more powerful and lasting than easy commercial success.

For you rock video trivia buffs, here's something. In "Holding Back the Years" there are several shots of a large ruined structure. These are the ruins of Whitby Abbey, which figures prominently in the original *Dracula*, by Bram Stoker. Indeed, much of the video was shot in and around the northern England seaside town of Whitby, where much of the action of *Dracula* was also set.

To contact Simply Red write:

Elektra Records
665 Fifth Avenue
New York, NY 10022

EL DEBARGE

With his first solo album and, particularly, with his extremely popular video for "Who's Johnny," from the soundtrack of the movie *Short Circuit,* El DeBarge appears ready to make the move into major solo stardom. But some fans wonder what happened to the family group DeBarge. El insists that there's no feud.

"I started my solo career because there's so much talent in my family. My brothers and sisters needed this space to get some attention. When people have talent, they want to be recognized for it, they want people to know about it. Now there's a lot more space for them to do what they need to do. Bunny's recording her own solo LP, and so is Chico."

The DeBarge family is large, and close-knit. El is one of ten children born in Detroit, but he

El DeBarge
(Courtesy The Howard Bloom Organization)

grew up in Grand Rapids, Michigan. The family was poor, and El often tells how during the winter they wore old socks instead of gloves. But they were rich in musical talent. Says El, "I wrote my first song when I was five. My older brother Bobby and sister Bunny organized a singing group with me when I was six. We sang songs my mother wrote for us."

They sang other songs as well. El's mother recalled, "I would wake up the oldest five children real early, like six o'clock in the morning, to sing on radio gospel programs. They sang songs like 'Little David Play On Your Harp' and 'Gospel Train.' "

Detroit was hard on the DeBarge family. Grand Rapids was much better. "When we moved to Grand Rapids," says El, "we had a lot of relatives that moved up there from different parts of the world and it was almost like a family reunion, almost as if God said, 'This is where I want the family to get together.' "

El's uncle was pastor of the Bethel Pentecostal Church, and his uncle was the minister of music, so naturally the family had many chances to sing in the church. "I played organ, my brothers Randy and James played bass, Bobby and I played keyboards, Marty played trumpet, and all of us—including Bunny—sang. We were a famous choir in the gospel circuit: the Bethel Pentecostal Choir."

El's oldest brothers, Bobby and Tommy, were the first to go beyond gospel. They went to Los Angeles and formed a group called Switch. As they tell the story, they were riding in an elevator in the Motown building in Los Angeles and met Jermaine Jackson. They gave him a tape, and he loved it. So Switch signed with Motown.

It was several years before El himself tried to get into the record business. "I was afraid of L.A." But when he was sixteen, he went out to visit his brothers. He and his sister Bunny went to meet them in the Motown building. They hoped to audition too, but no one seemed interested in hearing them. While they were waiting, El sat down at a piano and started playing. Bunny began to sing. And once again Jermaine Jackson just happened to be there. Jermaine loved what he heard. "And we had to come back the next day and do it all over again for every single department head. And that's how DeBarge got started with Motown."

It was a year before DeBarge produced any records. They wanted to develop their own style, write their own material. But as soon as the records started coming out they started selling. By the time DeBarge went on its first tour in 1983, the group already had a large following.

When El decided to strike out on his own a

lot of the old DeBarge fans were upset. They were also upset at a new DeBarge "sound." But El realizes that in music, as in life, you can't stand still. The new El DeBarge is attracting a wider audience than ever.

What's next? El has been so successful with his video that he's been thinking of taking up acting.

"I definitely want to try acting, but I'm not foolish enough to think I can just walk through it." This extremely talented young man is looking for new worlds to conquer.

To contact El DeBarge write:

Motown Record Corp.
6255 Sunset Boulevard
Los Angeles, CA 90028

SIMPLE MINDS

In rock, success is sometimes just as hard to take as failure. There are enough tragic stories about major rock stars whose lives simply dissolved. The trick is staying sane and whole.

"This life," says Jim Kerr of Simple Minds, "is like a gold mountain. You've got to keep one foot on it and the rest off."

The members of Simple Minds appear to be handling their new-found success very well. Perhaps that's because it didn't come to them overnight. While they are only in their twenties, the two primary members of the band—Jim Kerr and Charlie Burchill—have been working together for nearly ten years. They've been friends since grade school.

Kerr and Burchill grew up in a working-class

Simple Minds
(Courtesy A&M Records)

district in the very working-class city of Glasgow, Scotland. Kerr recalls sneaking into Pink Floyd and Led Zeppelin concerts when he was a teenager. Kerr and Burchill started with a punk band in 1977, but that type of music soon began to bore them. Kerr calls it "hokey," and a "con game." "No one was threatened because of a haircut."

In 1978, Kerr and Burchill recruited seventeen-year-old Mick MacNeil, another Glasgow boy, to form Simple Minds. Like practically all bands, they have gone through changes over the years. Drummer Mel Gaynor was added in 1983 and more recently bassist John Giblin, vocalist Robin Clark, and percussionist Sue Hadjopulos have joined.

Simple Minds built up a fairly solid following in Scotland and England after just a few years, but they failed to click on their first American tour. They seemed to have settled into the status of a cult band. Then, in 1985, the group's "Don't You (Forget About Me)" began topping the charts in the U.S. At that time Simple Minds was holed up in Scotland, and though they heard about their success, they weren't fully aware of what it meant until their 1986 U.S. tour. Suddenly, there were trucks, road crews, and hordes of groupies hounding them for autographs after each performance. It's all been a bit embarrassing, particularly for a group which at one time seemed to scorn mass success.

Kerr has no apologies for Simple Minds' new fame. "There are no cult bands anymore. You're either commercial failures or commercial successes." But that doesn't mean that the band will pursue success at any cost. "We have to try and show that there's a side to this rock game other than just hamburger music. And if that means beating them at their own game, then we must beat them at their own game."

Kerr and Burchill both made a conscious effort not to let their success tear them away from their working-class roots in Glasgow. Kerr recalls painful moments when guys he had gone to school with would travel hundreds of miles to see one of his concerts, and then come up to him afterwards and say, "You don't remember me, but I used to go to school with you." Kerr would be astonished. "What are you talking about? How could I forget you?"

Kerr and Burchill credit a good deal of their own stability to their solid families, and to the strong sense of community which existed while they were growing up. Can such values survive in the fast-paced, ever-shifting world of rock? Jim Kerr wonders, for he is married to Chrissie Hynde of the Pretenders. They live in Edinburgh, Scotland, and have a two-year-old daughter, Yasmin. Since both Jim and Chrissie tour a lot with their respective bands, Kerr is concerned. "I don't know what will happen."

Both Kerr and Burchill are well aware of the personal dangers of rock success, but they feel that they've had enough experience, and a solid enough background, to avoid the pitfalls.

To contact Simple Minds write:

A&M Records
1416 North La Brea Avenue
Hollywood, CA 90028

U2

"Not even Bruce Springsteen could claim to have a more loyal following than U2," says rock writer Adam Sweeting. That's quite a statement. And it's probably true.

The members of U2—Bono (vocals), Dave "The Edge" Evans (guitar and piano), Larry Mullen (drums), and Adam Clayton (bass)—met and formed the group in 1978, while attending school in Dublin, Ireland. From the start, U2 was determined to go its own way and play their own kind of music, no matter what the trends and fashions. If people didn't like what they were doing, that was just too bad, as far as U2 was concerned.

In fact, the group was quite successful with critics and knowledgeable rock fans almost from the start. They never had, or looked for,

Bono of U2 at the Amnesty International Concert
(John Bellissimo)

U2

the sort of mass success of a Duran Duran or Wham! But they did build up a loyal following, first in Europe and later in America.

U2 isn't your basic good-time, party band. It's a group of deep commitment, even spirituality. One of their best numbers, "Pride (In The Name Of Love)," is a passionate tribute to Martin Luther King and everyone who has sacrificed and died in the name of love.

Over the past few years, a lot of rock groups have contributed their time and talents to a variety of good causes, from African famine relief to helping the American farmer. U2 has contributed more than most. The Irish group was one of the prime movers behind the very successful "Conspiracy of Hope" concerts for the human rights organization, Amnesty International. When Jack Healey, executive director of Amnesty International USA, began planning the Amnesty concerts, he went to Dublin to see U2 first. Healey knew the group would be sympathetic. They agreed to the project almost instantly.

Understand that this was not an agreement to participate in a single concert or recording session. It was an agreement to do at least a week of concerts in June, usually the height of the touring season for rock groups. It meant rearranged schedules, broken commitments, and the loss of a great deal of money for U2.

But they did it anyway, without a hassle, because it was something they believed in. With U2 on board, a lot of other top names in rock joined up to make the "Conspiracy of Hope" tour a great success.

U2 has never acted like other bands. For years band members wouldn't even talk to reporters. Even today they don't do a lot of talking, and they don't turn up a lot in fan magazine gossip. You get the idea that the only reason that they give interviews now is so the fact that they *don't* give interviews won't become an issue. Yet their popularity has continued to grow. A critics' poll in 1983 voted U2 the band of the year; the magazine, *The Record,* named them best live act of the year. And in 1985, *Rolling Stone* magazine called U2, "The Band of the '80s."

The band's album *War* was so popular that U2 is almost embarrassed by it. "We will probably never make a record like *War* again," says The Edge. Their next album, *The Unforgettable Fire,* is much more difficult. Even record company publicists described it as "raw, seeming almost undefined." It's not easy listening. But *The Unforgettable Fire* has also proved to be enormously popular.

Not too many years ago, a lot of rock performers thought of videos as a nuisance. A group like U2 would not have bothered with videos, or at least would not have taken much trouble making them. All that's different now. Videos are almost universally regarded as a legitimate art form. So it's not entirely surprising that a group like U2 would produce some of the most dynamic and moving videos made in recent years.

To contact U2 write:

Island Records, Inc.
14 East Fourth Street
New York, NY 10012

TOM PETTY AND THE HEARTBREAKERS

In 1979, before there was such a thing as MTV, Tom Petty and the Heartbreakers were already thinking video. The band created innovative videos for the songs "Refugee" and "Here Comes My Girl" from their hit album *Damn The Torpedoes*. They did this at a time when many musicians balked at making videos or considered them unimportant. The group's next album, *Hard Promises,* spawned what was then an unprecedented four videos. So it was only to be expected that once videos emerged as a major new medium, Tom and the band would come up with something really ingenious. Their *Alice in Wonderland* style video of "Don't Come Around Here No More" is pure gold.

This video version of the mad tea party is

Tom Petty
(Courtesy Lookout Management)

mad indeed, with Tom, in real life a very nice guy, decked out as a rather sinister Mad Hatter. The video has dazzling imagery, beautiful color, and a delightful undertone of humor. "Don't Come Around Here No More" won all kinds of video awards, including the Grand Prize for Best Video Clip at Europe's Montreux Golden Rose Television Festival, and the MTV Award for Best Special Effects. The band has gone right on using video with flair.

The original home of Tom Petty and the guys who would some day become the Heartbreakers is northern Florida, an area which includes Gainesville and Jacksonville. Their southern background shows up in album titles like *Southern Accents* and *Pack Up The Plantation*. It shows up in their music, too, even though the band has undergone some changes since then. For example, bassist Howie Epstein is from Milwaukee, Wisconsin.

Tom was a teenager when he and a group of friends formed a locally popular Florida band called Mudcrutch. Eventually Mudcrutch dissolved and its members all went their separate ways. It turned out that their separate ways followed the same road, straight to California. While pursuing their dreams in Los Angeles, they met again, got together and started playing music. The group realized that together they formed the band of their dreams and that they need look no further. So they changed their name to Tom Petty and the Heartbreakers, launched a debut record of the same name and started playing clubs. They also toured, opening for Al Kooper and later for Cheap Trick.

Like many home-grown groups before and since, they had their first big success in Britain, where their album and single of *Anything That's Rock n' Roll* hit the British top twenty. After that, it was home to America, where albums and records rang up gold and platinum. The group has shown a sense of commitment by performing at Live Aid and Farm Aid. It was at Farm Aid that they first worked with the legendary Bob Dylan, later touring with him. Tom Petty and the Heartbreakers have come a long way since they were kids in Florida. World famous, they're one of the hottest bands around.

To contact Tom Petty and the Heartbreakers write:

MCA Records
100 Universal City Plaza
Universal City, CA 16078

HUEY LEWIS AND THE NEWS

Sometimes you may feel that Huey Lewis and the News have been around forever. Other times it seems as if they came suddenly out of nowhere. In fact, there is a good deal of truth in both statements.

Lewis grew up in Marin County, California with what he has called "authentically Bohemian," that is unconventional, parents. His father was a jazz drummer and doctor. His mother was an artist who painted flowers on the wall of the old Filmore Auditorium. Lewis attended a fancy East Coast prep school. But after graduation, he took his father's suggestion, learned to play the harmonica and hitchhiked across Europe.

Huey Lewis really got his start in music in the San Francisco Bay area, as the harmonica

Huey Lewis
(Courtesy Chrysalis)

player with Clover, a country-rock group. The group cut a few records with a small label, but the records went nowhere. However, Clover had developed a following in England, so they moved there and recorded a few more albums. The timing was bad for country-rock. Clover arrived in England at the height of the punk-rock explosion.

Clover broke up and Lewis drifted back to California. He started playing in Monday night jam sessions at a little bar in California called Uncle Charlie's. Years later, Lewis would return to Uncle Charlie's to shoot the video for "The Power of Love." The group that gathered at Uncle Charlie's was to form the nucleus for Huey Lewis and the News.

The group finally got a record contract. The band's debut album in 1980 was a modest success. In 1982 they recorded a second album, *Sports*. This album sat unreleased on a shelf for nine months, while the band toured small clubs, singing songs from an album nobody had ever heard. Despite the long delay before the album was finally released, it turned into a major success.

But there were two events that turned Huey Lewis and the News into authentic rock superstars. The first was the "We Are The World" record and video. Lewis appeared alongside Michael Jackson, Bruce Springsteen, and the other royalty of the rock world. He looked like he belonged there.

Lewis and the News also contributed a live recording of their song "Trouble in Paradise" to the *We Are The World* album, and that brought the band's music to a larger audience than ever before. Benefits like USA for Africa can not only raise funds for charity, they can sometimes do a great deal for the performers who contribute their talent.

The second event which boosted the band to superstar status was their connection with the immensely popular Steven Spielberg hit *Back to the Future*. Lewis and the News sang "Power of Love," which went on to become the band's biggest hit ever. The video for "Power of Love" was the band's most popular video. Lewis and the News also performed "Back in Time" for the film, and Lewis himself even played a small part in the movie. This is not so much an example of the "Power of Love" but of the Power of Movies and Movie Videos, in advancing the fortunes of a band.

At one time, the only way a band could become known was through touring. Lewis and the News have certainly been doing plenty of that. In three consecutive years of playing New Year's Eve in the Bay Area, the band moved from the 700-seat Old Waldorf, to the 1400-seat Kabuki Theatre, to the 14,000-seat

Oakland Coliseum Arena. They have sold out arenas from New York to New Zealand. Huey Lewis and the News have had cable TV specials, magazine covers, Grammy nominations—all the advantages that come with success.

And practically everybody agrees that it really couldn't happen to a nicer guy.

"That's really the secret," Lewis told interviewers David and Victoria Sheff. "It has nothing to do with the record or the fact that we're a good band or the videos. It's just that I'm a nice guy."

To contact Huey Lewis and the News write:

Chrysalis Records Inc.
645 Madison Avenue
New York, NY 10022

MR. MISTER

Mr. Mister is a thoroughly professional, thoroughly modern, and thoroughly California band.

Richard Page and Steve George, the two central figures of Mr. Mister, didn't come from California originally. They grew up together in Phoenix, Arizona. As teenagers, they played in various local bands. But Phoenix is not a music center, so in 1975 Richard and Steve headed for Los Angeles to try and make it in the big time. Not only did the pair manage to survive in the tough competitive music market (and smog) of Southern California, they began to thrive. And they began to think about forming their own group.

Steve Farris also came from somewhere else—from Nebraska in his case. Steve made

Mr. Mister
(© Gregg Gorman, courtesy RCA Records)

his way to California, where he starved and struggled for years until he started playing with Eddie Money. That lasted three years. In 1982, Richard and Steve George were holding auditions for a new band they were forming. They hit it off immediately with Steve Farris, and he has since become an integral part of the Mr. Mister songwriting team.

Pat Mastelotto was born in Northern California. He reckons he has played with every local band in the San Fernando Valley. He is a serious drummer who doesn't talk much. "I play drums. Hard," he says simply.

Mr. Mister

The four musicians knew their business, and soon Mr. Mister had developed its own very distinctive sound. It has been described as "white rhythm and blues." Mr. Mister first began appearing in public in the spring of 1982. Within a couple of months they had signed a record contract with RCA.

Their first album, *I Wear The Face*, released in the spring of 1984, was a modest, but not overwhelming success. Still, it got the band's name known, and promised better things for the future.

The band decided that in order to get the sort of sound they wanted, they would have to have complete control of production. Most people outside the music business don't realize it, but the mixer or engineer who controls the machinery of recording can be every bit as important as the musicians in determining what a record sounds like. Professionals, like the members of Mr. Mister, do realize the importance of the engineer, and they were very careful in choosing one.

In the end they chose a relative newcomer, Paul De Villiers. "This guy was fresh, eager, not L.A.'d out. It felt right," said Steve Farris. The result of months of intensive work in the studio was the album *Welcome to the Real World*.

A few exciting videos helped to move the album right up the charts, and establish Mr. Mister as one of the solidly popular favorites of rock today.

To contact Mr. Mister write:

RCA Records
6363 Sunset Boulevard
Hollywood, CA 90028

JANET JACKSON

"My name ain't baby—it's Janet, or Miss Jackson, if you're nasty."

That's a line from the Janet Jackson hit, "Nasty," but it's more than just a song lyric. It expresses just exactly what has happened to Janet. In fact, her whole hit album, *Control,* is a reflection of a new and much tougher Janet Jackson.

"A lot has happened to me in the past year and a half . . ." says Janet. "I've experienced a great deal, and I'm much the wiser for it. I'm making decisions for myself. 'Control' is the song that really relates my feelings these days, and I didn't pull any punches on that song or any other."

Janet is, of course, the youngest sister of the incredibly famous and talented Jackson clan.

Janet Jackson
(Courtesy A&M Records)

She first began appearing onstage with her brothers when she was only seven. She did cute kiddie imitations of Mae West and Cher. By age ten she was doing TV shows like "Good Times" and "Different Strokes." She also cut a couple of solo albums, *Janet Jackson* in 1982, and *Dream Street* in 1984. But inevitably she remained "the baby" and was in the shadow of her older brothers, who helped both produce and write her albums.

Control is a very different sort of production, and the title is no accident, "When I've made records in the past," Janet explains, "I've usually been given a tape of a song, learned it, and then gone into the studio and sung to a completed instrumental track. This time around, I intend to be completely involved in the recording process, from the songwriting to the playing to the production."

For this album she has done just about everything. She is co-producer, she shared the songwriting duties, and she plays keyboards and synthesizers on the majority of the tracks.

The songs, like "Nasty," "Control," and "What Have You Done for Me Lately," are absolutely straightforward. "People will be shocked when they hear 'Control,' " Janet has said, "because it's so different from what I've done before. But I think they'll like it. This is a very special record to me—it expresses exactly who I am and how I feel. I've taken control of my own life."

Shocked is too strong a word to describe the reaction to "Control." People were, however, surprised, and we might add delighted. The video for "Nasty" reinforced the new Janet Jackson image—no longer Michael's cute little sister, but a tough and very talented young woman who is just at the start of a great solo career.

To contact Janet Jackson write:

A&M Records Inc.
1416 North La Brea Avenue
Hollywood, CA 90028

TEARS FOR FEARS

When you call yourself Tears For Fears and title your first album *The Hurting*, people may get the impression that you're not exactly a fun-loving group of guys. It's true. Tears For Fears don't make what you'd call "have-a-nice-day" music.

Yet the group was an early and solid success in both the U.S. and Britain. They have tried to combine good tunes with emotional depth. Their music is both moody and uplifting. Tears For Fears' stated goal was to create "music for the body, the heart, and the mind." That's a neat trick if you can do it. Tears For Fears has managed to pull it off. They have developed a strong cult following, are very popular with the critics, and have a growing audience among the general run of music fans as well.

Tears for Fears

Tears For Fears began quietly in Bath, England, where the two young men who make up the group were born. Curt Smith (vocals, bass) and Roland Orzabal (vocals, guitar, keyboards, and rhythm programming) have known each other since the age of thirteen, when they met at school in Bath. They formed their first band, called Graduate, when they were nineteen. It took a few years to perfect their sound (and change their name), but after that success followed success. Their first single in 1982, "Suffer The Children," actually got more attention in the East Coast U.S. dance clubs than it did back home in England. The single, "Mad World," was a hit in the U.K. and helped them to launch their first British tour. When *The Hurting* was released, the critics, who can be tigers, were purring like pussycats. Said *Rolling Stone:* "It is a testimony to their refined pop instincts that they manage to produce this much pleasure from the pain." *Stereo Review* called the album "a wonderful record and one of the real surprises of this year . . . *The Hurting* contains some of the most intelligent use of a synthesizer that I've come across." Said another critic, "Virtually alone among modern day synth bands, Tears For Fears is deep and unpretentious."

The little group with the unhappy name is one of the most interesting and original around. To contact Tears For Fears write:

Polygram Records
810 Seventh Avenue
New York, NY 10019

THE MOODY BLUES

What do you get when you put Justin Hayward on guitar, John Lodge on bass, Graeme Edge on drums, Ray Thomas on flute, and Patrick Moraz on keyboards? You get the Moody Blues, that's what, one of the most revered bands in rock. It's often here today, gone tomorrow with rock bands. Many a superstar disappears from sight after a year or two at the top. Yet the Moody Blues have had a loyal following of fans for ages, and their record sales are up in the stratosphere, with over forty million albums sold.

The Moody Blues
(Courtesy Concerts West)

The Moody Blues' first full studio album, *Days of Future Passed,* was released in (get this, rock buffs) 1967, yes, way back in the era of protest movements, mini-skirts, and psychedelic art. The lovely "Forever Afternoon (Tuesday)" from the album was a hit single then. Today the song's a classic. The Moody Blues followed up their success with a tour. From the very beginning, the Moody Blues have understood the importance of staying in close touch with their fans. Touring has become a way of life for them.

In 1968, after *In Search Of The Lost Chord* was released, the band toured America for the first time, playing to sold-out houses in big cities. Their concert tour took them to The Shrine in Los Angeles and the legendary Fillmore East in New York, as well as the Fillmore West in San Francisco. Gold and platinum albums kept right on coming, and in 1970, the Moodies, eager to obtain their own label identity, formed Threshold Records.

In 1972, six years after its initial success on the charts, the Moody Blues' classic "Nights In White Satin" was re-released in the United States. It stayed on the charts for months. "Nights In White Satin" returned to the British charts three separate times in the years that followed, making the top ten each time.

Not surprisingly, with that kind of track record, the Moody Blues were really hot in the early 1970s. In 1973, they went on a historic tour which took them across Europe, then on to Japan, Hawaii, and the United States. Then for a while it looked as if the Moodies might go their separate ways, a scary moment for millions of fans. Although the Moodies did not appear together for five years, they didn't split up or disappear. Justin and John collaborated

The Moody Blues

on an album called *Blue Jays* in 1975, and Graeme Edge made solo albums before taking a trip around the world on his ocean-going cruiser. Ray Thomas produced two solo albums during this period, and John's album, *Natural Avenue,* and Justin's album, *Songwriter,* were released in 1977. The only band member who left the group, never to return, was keyboard player Mike Pinder.

The mood was anything but blue in the world of rock when the Moody Blues returned as a group in 1978, with Patrick Moraz taking over for Pinder. Their very first album this time round was *Octave,* which easily soared into the top twenty. They were number one again with *Long Distance Voyager* in 1981, and from there it was one hit after another, each album generating popular singles.

How have the Moody Blues been able to stay together when so many other groups split apart? For one thing, they look after their own business interests, sharing rewards and responsibilities fairly. They refuse to churn out songs just to make money quickly, and take their time with recording schedules. They ignore trends, creating first of all for themselves, releasing only what they like. Not least, they've maintained their commitment to bringing live music to their fans via tours. Let other groups come and go. The Moody Blues are forever.

To contact the Moody Blues write:

Polygram Records
810 Seventh Avenue
New York, NY 10019

PETER GABRIEL

It was sixties' soul music that inspired Peter Gabriel's smash hit song, "Sledgehammer." The song is from his album *So* and was also released as a single. By the time it reached your television screen, "Sledgehammer" was a very exciting video, one of the best to come along in many a day, rich in color, detail, and motion. Of course, Peter Gabriel understands such things. He once considered going to film school and, though he opted for music instead of movies, he has a gift for visual imagery. He has ideas about videos, too, strong ones. To Peter, video is an art form still in its infancy. He'd like to see longer videos made, and videos which look less like commercials. So, since Peter likes to experiment with his ideas, he's been busily working with painters and sculp-

Peter Gabriel
(Trevor Key, courtesy Gailforce Management Ltd.)

tors in London and New York, encouraging them to explore video technology and to create new styles.

Born in 1950, Peter Gabriel has been writing songs since he was sixteen. Today he is considered one of the most intelligent and innovative persons in the world of rock music. Peter did not come from a working-class family, as so many British rock musicians do. He attended an elite school called Charterhouse in Surrey, England. Peter's family expected him to go to college, but he preferred to become part of a band called Genesis.

Peter Gabriel

The name Genesis spells success. It's one of the top bands around, although that wasn't always true. Peter and the other band members had their share of ups and downs getting started, especially since they were often viewed as "the rich kids" in the tough neighborhood of rock. When Peter left Genesis in 1975, it was Phil Collins who would take his place. Peter had been known for his theatricality when he was with Genesis, but once he went solo he changed, becoming more restrained, more versatile.

Peter's interest in experimental rock grew, and he became fascinated with the music of other cultures, especially African music. His songs often reflect his strong social conscience and liberal political views. For example, the song "Biko" is about Steve Biko, the murdered black South African activist, and the song "Mercy Street" reflects the influence feminist writer Anne Sexton has had on Peter.

Among Peter Gabriel's most important projects to date are his work on the soundtrack of Alan Parsons' critically acclaimed movie *Birdy,* and his help with the WOMAD Festival. WOMAD (World of Music Arts and Dance) first began in 1982 in a place called Shepton Mallet. It was started by Peter and some friends of his who published a record magazine called the *Bristol Recorder*. The festival involved musicians from over twenty-five countries and featured workshops, a children's parade, movies, theatre, and dance. Now a highly respected annual music event, WOMAD specializes in educational activities, and the WOMAD organization has released several multi-cultural records.

The latest creative project to sprout in the clever brain of Peter Gabriel is an amusement park, possibly slated for Sydney, Australia. It won't be like Disneyland: this theme park is to be called Real World. Artists of all kinds will be involved in its construction, and visitors will play a very active role in the park's exhibits. There won't be any simply riding along and looking at what's on display. Just as he immersed himself in music, Peter is equally immersed in what he calls "ludic art," the art of games, and he's got some fabulous games planned for his theme park. Multi-talented, that's Peter Gabriel. What will he think of next?

To contact Peter Gabriel write:

Geffen Records
75 Rockefeller Plaza
New York, NY 10010

THE FAT BOYS

Tired of all those super-thin Mick Jagger, Michael Jackson look-alikes? Welcome a group of real substance—the Fat Boys.

These young rappers originally called themselves Disco 3. During an early European tour, their manager was presented with a bill for $350 for "extra breakfasts." The manager complained that they should call themselves the Fat Boys. Their hilarious video—a celebration of overeating—became unofficially known as "the Fat Boys' video." So they officially changed their name. It seemed the natural thing to do.

The Brooklyn-born teenagers who make up the Fat Boys are Darren "The Human Beat Box" Robinson, Mark "Prince Markie Dee" Morales, and Damon "Kool Rock-ski"

The Fat Boys
(Raeanne Rubenstein, courtesy Tin Pan Apple)

Wimbley. They were first noticed outside of Brooklyn when they made the finals of the Tin Pan Apple Rap Contest held at Radio City Music Hall in May of 1983. Since then it's been onward and upward.

The Fat Boys are beginning to collect an impressive number of gold records. They have been headlining sold-out U.S. and European tours. But it's on video that these comic rappers really shine. They have already made seven of them, including "All You Can Eat." The videos have proved so popular that they have released "Fat Boys on Video: Brrr, Watch 'Em!," a collection of video favorites of the hefty trio.

The Fat Boys have made guest appearances on many television shows, from "Sixty Minutes" to "Miami Vice." And they had show-stealing roles in the rap film, "Krush Groove." There are at least three more Fat Boys films now under contract. But the Fat Boys have probably received most exposure as the spokesmen for Swatch watches, appearing in a number of highly praised and wonderfully comic commercials.

Though the Fat Boys project an image of pure fun-loving hilarity, they are not unaffected by what has been happening in the world around them. And they have been willing to dedicate their time and talents to help a variety of causes. They have appeared at the Sun City anti-apartheid benefit and the Martin Luther "King Holiday." In fact, they officially changed their name to the Fat Boys while appearing at a fundraiser for the United Negro College Fund.

To contact the Fat Boys write:

Tin Pan Apple, Inc.
1790 Broadway, 18th Floor
New York, NY 10019

a-ha

Oslo, Norway isn't exactly the center of the rock 'n' roll world. It isn't even the suburbs. It's more like the outskirts. So when a couple of ambitious young Norwegian rock 'n' rollers named Pal (pronounced Paul) Waataar and Magne Furuholmen (fortunately better known simply as Mags) decided they wanted to be stars, they took off for the hotbed of the London music scene.

While in London, Paul and Mags tried to form a group using English musicians. The attempt failed. "It just wasn't working," explains Mags, "but it was a really exciting time in London. A lot of new things were happening on the charts and we really got inspired. We realized that we had the opportunity to do something different and have it accepted."

a-ha
(Robert Erdmann)

Pal and Mags returned to Norway after six months. They had a plan to form a new band. They knew just who they wanted to round out the planned group, vocalist Morten Harket. In fact, they had tried to persuade Morten to come to London with them, but he was given very short notice and he declined. Now Pal and Mags decided to try again. This time their persuasiveness worked.

In January of 1983, Pal and Mags returned to London with Morten in tow and began making the rounds of record company offices with a series of homemade demos. It was a discouraging process. Mags actually had to return to Oslo to earn money to finance the making of more demos.

But luck finally smiled on this good-looking trio. While doing some recording at London's Rendezvous Studios, they happened to be overheard by some important people in the record business. These important people introduced them to some other important people, and soon a-ha had a recording contract with Warner Brothers Records.

Part of a-ha's appeal is their crisp, innovative and danceable sound. But part is also due to the fact that this is the hottest looking trio to come down the pike in a long time. Because appearance is so important, a-ha has taken exceptional care with its videos. The group is not content to use the same visual effects which have become clichés over the last few years. Their video for the hit single "Take On Me" was an original blending of live action and cartoons, making it one of the best and most exciting videos of recent history. The video took a flock of nominations and awards at the 1986 MTV Awards. The members of a-ha were honored as best new artists. The group also kicked off its first U.S. tour in mid 1986.

While the members of a-ha have not exactly had an unbroken rise to success, they have not had to endure some of the hardships that other groups have suffered. Mags, Pal, and Morten all come from relatively well-off backgrounds.

Mags's father was a musician, who was

killed in a plane crash. His mother was a teacher. Before becoming a rock musician, Mags held a number of different jobs, including working in a mental hospital, a duty he performed as part of his alternative service. (In Norway, when a man refuses to do military service, he may be given some sort of job in a social agency such as a mental hospital.) Mags, like the other members of a-ha, is a conscientious objector. In fact, Mags and Morten wound up working in the same mental hospital.

Pal, the quietest member of the trio, comes from a highly respectable family. His father is a research scientist, his mother an administrator. They thought that music was an interesting hobby, but figured that one day Pal would grow out of it. He never did.

Morten's father is a doctor, his mother a teacher. He has an older brother who is a journalist and a sister who's a painter. But all Morten could ever dream about was being a rock star. In fact, he did so poorly in school that it looked as if he would have to be a rock star or nothing.

To contact a-ha write:

Warner Bros. Records Inc.
3300 Warner Boulevard
Burbank, CA 91510

DIRE STRAITS

In 1977, the original Dire Straits scraped together $180 to make their first ever demo recording. One of the songs, titled "Sultans of Swing," is the story of a band whose members had to stand on the breadline in order to get enough to eat. They played for love and dreamed of better days. The song is the real account of what happened to the group. At that time, Dire Straits were in dire straits themselves.

Over the years a lot has changed. The better days they dreamed of have arrived. The group has released five albums, which have sold over seventeen million copies worldwide. There have been changes in the makeup of Dire Straits, and there have been long periods when members of the band have gone off to pursue

Dire Straits
(David Bailey, courtesy Damage Management)

individual projects. But when they do get together, in the studio or on the stage, as they did in 1986 after almost two years of being apart, they are still a dynamite group, with the same distinct Dire Straits sound. The group's video "Money for Nothin' " took the top prize at the 1986 MTV Awards.

Dire Straits founder, lead singer, guitarist, and chief songwriter Mark Knopfler had not been idle while he was away from the group. Among other projects, he has worked with a wonderful Scottish director named Bill Forsyth—whose films are not nearly well known enough in the U.S.—on the film *Comfort and Joy*.

A lot of musicians who have tried working in movies have hated the experience. Knopfler was different—he loved it. "Being a singer and songwriter is a pretty selfish occupation in many ways," he says. "You please yourself. One of the nice things about film music is that it is designed to support and enhance somebody else's vision. That aspect of it appealed to me greatly."

Perhaps it's Mark's association with films that has made Dire Straits so attentive to the quality of their videos. Most groups are personally involved in the sound of their recordings, but leave their videos in the control of others, sometimes with unhappy results. Dire

Dire Straits

Straits is as careful about videos as they are about records. As a result, their videos have a consistent originality and freshness.

John Illsley, bass guitarist, who along with Mark was one of the founding members of Dire Straits, released his first solo album recently. The entire group, with the exception of Mark, played on Tina Turner's extremely popular version of "Private Dancer." Mark himself wrote the song.

With members of Dire Straits pursuing so many solo projects, it might seem that the group's future was in doubt. Many other groups have broken up when members went in search of greener pastures. But this doesn't appear to be happening with Dire Straits. The members are now committed to group projects for the next couple of years. Their many fans couldn't be happier about that news.

To contact Dire Straits write:

Warner Bros. Records, Inc.
3300 Warner Boulevard
Burbank, CA 91510

JACKSON BROWNE

When Jackson Browne first started touring in the late 1960s, he traveled with his guitar and a suitcase. On his latest tour, he had a bus, a couple of trucks, and tons of electronic equipment. But basically, after twenty years, it's still the same Jackson Browne. And that's very good news for the legion of Browne fans who had feared that one of rock's leading composers and poets had somehow lost his way.

In his early years Browne was regarded as a typical California folksinger. Actually, Browne was born in Heidelberg, West Germany, but he grew up in California. He was one of the founding members of the country-rock band, The Nitty Gritty Dirt Band, which started a whole new musical style. By the early 1970s,

Jackson Browne
(Henry Diltz, courtesy Elektra/Asylum)

Browne was widely regarded as the socially committed successor to Bob Dylan, the musician/poet of the turbulent 1960s.

However, during the 1970s, a lot of things happened to Jackson Browne. A number of people who were close to him, including his first wife, died. He also found himself transformed from a "folkie" who could stand alone on a stage and sing, into a genuine rock star. Now he had to play to huge halls, rather than small rooms. He was also making a lot of money.

Some diehard Browne fans began to think that he had completely given in to the image of being a cool rock superstar, and was no longer interested in social issues. There was some suggestion that Browne had "sold out." Old-time fans were particularly outraged with his song "Somebody's Baby," written for the film *Fast Times at Ridgemont High*.

Browne insists that some of the songs that upset his fans were just funny, not meant to be taken seriously at all. The fact is that Jackson Browne was just as deeply committed to the causes he believed in as ever before. He gave away a lot of the money he made. It's just that "causes" for rock stars weren't that popular in the 1970s and early 1980s.

Times change. Starting with Band Aid and Live Aid, and all of the other benefit concerts

Jackson Browne at the Amnesty International Concert
(© 1986 Barry Morgenstein/MWA)

given by rock performers, commitment to social causes is "in" again. Of course, Jackson Browne didn't have to wait for fashion. He had been there all the time. His appearance at the gigantic Amnesty International concert at the Meadowlands in New Jersey was one of the high points of that star-studded day. When he sang, the thousands in the stands and the millions watching on television knew it was from the heart. It was the sort of sincerity that can't be faked. Jackson Browne's passion for social justice is the real thing.

Browne's latest album, *Lives In the Balance,* is one of his biggest hits yet. It's popular with old-time Browne fans and newcomers as well. Rock critics hailed "the return of Jackson Browne." The creative dry spell which afflicted him for several years seems to be over. Wrote Lydia Carole DeFretos: "While every other artist around is jumping on the 'Ethiopia bandwagon' leave it to Browne to pinpoint the troubles at home."

Some of Browne's videos, as well as some of his live appearances, like the Amnesty International concert, have been brightened by the appearance of his girlfriend, the actress Daryl Hannah. In case you don't know the name, she was the mermaid in the film *Splash*.

To contact Jackson Browne write:

Elektra Records
75 Rockefeller Plaza
New York, NY 10019

THE MONKEES

It's the late 1960s. The Beatle craze is at its height. The Beatles' film, *A Hard Day's Night,* is a smash. Some TV producers get a bright idea. Why not do a comedy show about the antics of a Beatles-type singing group? The producers don't have any particular group in mind, so they decide to form one. They auditioned some singers, musicians, and actors, and wound up with Davy Jones, Micky Dolenz, Peter Tork, and Michael Nesmith. Davy and Micky were actors, Peter and Michael musicians. The group was dubbed the Monkees.

The show began with the Monkees theme song:

"Hey, hey, we're the Monkees, and people say we monkey around, but we're too busy singin' to put anybody down."

The show was fast, funny, upbeat, and very popular for two seasons. What's more, the group, although it was created artificially, with the band members not even playing their own instruments, evolved into a real band. Some of their songs, like "I'm a Believer," still hold up very well. The Monkees were recording albums for years after their show went off the air.

But that's history now. Or is it?

Suddenly, in 1986, the Monkees were making a big comeback. It wasn't just nostalgia either. The Monkees appeal to a lot of kids who weren't even born when the group first broke up.

The big push for the Monkees revival came from MTV. The channel started running the old shows, and discovered that there was a strong audience for the Monkees among regular MTV viewers. MTV even did a 22-hour Monkee marathon, which was a big hit.

So the Monkees were back. Actually, they never entirely went away. The group disbanded officially in 1970. Reruns of the original programs have been in syndication for years. Many of the Monkees' nine albums have remained in print, though they were increasingly hard to find. There was some talk of a reunion for a tour in 1975, but the deal never went through.

The Monkees
(John Bellissimo)

In the years since the Monkees broke up, Davy Jones moved back to his native England, and continued his career as an actor. Micky Dolenz, who was born in California, has recently relocated in England. He's been working there as a TV director and producer. He was also a voice on Saturday morning TV shows like "Scooby Doo" and "Funky Phantom." Peter Tork was a folksinger before he joined up with the Monkees. At the time of the revival, he was living in New York City and had been holding a variety of singing jobs. He was also said to be writing a book on the Monkees.

When the Monkees revival hit, producers

came up with the idea of reuniting the group for a major summer 1986 tour—doing all the old Monkees hits. The Monkees were, after all, the first real video band. Davy, Micky, and Peter loved the idea. And so the nationwide tour was launched.

But wait a minute, there were four Monkees. The fourth was Texan Michael Nesmith. He was the most accomplished musician when he joined the bunch. Michael has moved on to become one of the most influential figures in the world of rock video, and a pioneer of the long form video LP. He decided not to join the tour.

Is this to be a one-time tour? Davy, Micky, and Peter intend to pursue their separate careers. But no one is ruling out the possibility that the Monkees may be back yet again.

To contact the Monkees write:

Arista Records Inc.
Arista Building
6 West 57th Street
New York, NY 10019

GEORGE MICHAEL

Once he was a fat kid with glasses from the London suburb of Bushey who did nothing but listen to music. Once he was named Georgios Kyriacou Panoyiotu and nicknamed Yog. But that was a long time ago. He has since been transformed into one of rock's sexiest stars. He, of course, is George Michael, formerly one half of the phenomenally successful group, Wham!, now launched on his solo career.

George and fellow schoolmate at the Bushey Meads Secondary School, Andrew Ridgeley, formed their first band, the Executives, in 1979 when they were both sixteen. The following year, they adopted a West Indies sound and changed their name to Wham!, and after that their rise to the top was spectacular.

There had never been any doubt that George

was the dominant member of the group. When he started doing solo projects, rumors began to fly that Wham! would soon be no more. The split seems to have been amiable enough. Wham! gave a terrific farewell concert to a sell-out crowd at London's Wembley Stadium. The video made at that concert is a fine example of what a good concert video should be.

Now that George Michael is "goin' solo" where will he go?

George always said that it was Andrew who put a certain humor and "edge" into the Wham! performance. In his solo projects so far, George hasn't used the energetic Wham! sound, but concentrated on mellow songs, like the old Elton John classic, "Don't Let The Sun Go Down On Me," which he sang at the Live Aid concert.

Will a mellow George Michael be able to hold the millions of Wham! fans, and pick up new ones on his own? We're betting that he will.

To contact George Michael write:

Columbia Records
51 West 52nd Street
New York, NY 10019

George Michael
(Walter McBride/Retna Ltd.)

FILMS, COMICS, AND MUSCLEMEN

The old-time comedian Jimmy Durante used the line, "Everybody wants to get into the act!" Well, Durante could certainly say that about videos.

In their very early days, videos were called promos. They were put out by record companies to promote the sales of new records. Not too many people in the business took them seriously. They were made quickly and cheaply. But pretty soon the bands and the record company bigwigs found out that the public loved videos. Five years ago, a 24-hour-a-day music video network called MTV started. It has proved to be the greatest success story in cable television. The success of a record often depends on the quality of the videos. Some artists, like Madonna, Cyndi

Lauper, and Wham!, were *made* by videos. It's hard now for any record to be successful without a good video.

Now everybody wants to get into the video act. The biggest plunge has been made by Hollywood. Movies and music go back a long way together. In the past, lots of hit songs came from films. Later, soundtrack albums from films became popular. Then came the videos.

Today it seems as if the studios can't put out a film without at least one video. This is particularly true for films aimed at teens. In a recent Top 20 Video Countdown from MTV, fully one-third of the videos were from movies.

Frankly, we have found many movie videos disappointing. Clips from the film are alternated with performance shots of the artist. The result can be confusing and boring. The music and the pictures don't have anything to do with each other. Many of these videos look like cheap advertising.

Not all movie videos, however, are of poor quality. In some the performances or the music is so good that it overcomes all the limitations. For example, 38 Special's driving version of the title song for the film *Teachers* was very effective. It was better than the film itself! John Taylor's video for "I Do What I Do," from the film *Nine and a Half Weeks,* benefited not only

Billy Crystal
(Courtesy A&M Records)

from John's performance and music, but from some very exciting gymnastic shots from the film. The video was a hit. The film was not.

Comedians have also been getting into the video act. A lot of music videos are funny. Weird Al Yankovic has made a career doing musical parodies of popular rock videos. But "real" comedians have been making their own

Films, Comics, and Musclemen

videos too. Rodney Dangerfield did his "no respect" act to music, in a well-produced, and very funny, video, called "Rappin Rodney." More recently, Billy Crystal has turned his single, "You Look Marvelous," into a delightful video. Naturally, Billy appears as Fernando. But he also portrays Tina Turner, Prince, Grace Jones, and Sammy Davis, Jr. "Of course, I wanted to be funny," Billys says. "But I also wanted to be musical and danceable, and I think we pulled it off."

We think so, too. And we also think that you can expect lots more videos from comedians in the future.

But perhaps the most unusual new videos are the sports videos. It may have started with the rock 'n' wrestling connection. You remember back in 1985 when rock star Cyndi Lauper put wrestling manager Captain Lou Albano in some of her videos. Then she began managing a wrestler. A whole drama was played out on MTV and at Madison Square Garden.

But the wrestlers and wrestling promoters were not content to just be background in videos. They made their own. They employed the services of the portly rocker Meatloaf and his band, and they gathered together a few dozen of the biggest, strangest-looking people you have ever seen. Musically it wasn't so hot. Wrestlers can't sing. But they did end the show

Cyndi Lauper, her manager Dave Wolff, and Hulk Hogan
(John Bellissimo)

by throwing one another around and breaking up everything in sight. We guess you can say it was a smash.

The World Wrestling Federation also initiated its own music awards for wrestlers. They are called the Slammys.

The surprise sports video hit was made by a football team, the Chicago Bears, just before the 1986 Super Bowl. The likes of hot-dog quarterback Jim McMahon and the gigantic William "the Refrigerator" Perry teamed up to do a video called "The Super Bowl Shuffle." It proved to be so popular that the Bears' opponents, the New England Patriots, tried a video of their own. However, the Patriots' low-budget effort looked homemade compared to the Bears' very professional job. The Patriots were crushed in the Super Bowl too. In the late summer of 1986, the New York Mets who were running away with the National League East, made a video that was very popular, at least in New York.

What's next? Videos from boxers? Will we see Larry Bird singing? Who knows? The video world seems unlimited.

About the Authors

DANIEL COHEN is the author of over a hundred books for both young readers and adults, including some titles he has co-authored with his wife Susan. Among their popular titles are: *Supermonsters; The Greatest Monsters in the World; Real Ghosts; Ghostly Terrors; Science Fiction's Greatest Monsters; The World's Most Famous Ghosts; The Monsters of Star Trek; Rock Video Superstars; Rock Video Superstars II; Wrestling Superstars; Wrestling Superstars II;* and *Young and Famous: Hollywood's Newest Superstars;* all of which are available in Archway Paperback editions.

A former managing editor of *Science Digest* Magazine, Mr. Cohen was born in Chicago and has a degree in journalism from the University of Illinois. He appears frequently on radio and television, and has lectured at colleges and universities throughout the country. He lives with his wife, young daughter, one dog and four cats in Port Jervis, New York.

**Fast-paced, action-packed stories—
the ultimate adventure/mystery series!**

COMING SOON . . .
HAVE YOU SEEN
THE HARDY BOYS LATELY?

Beginning in April 1987, all-new Hardy Boys mysteries will be available in pocket-sized editions called THE HARDY BOYS CASEFILES.

Frank and Joe Hardy are eighties guys with eighties interests, living in Bayport, U.S.A. Their extracurricular activities include girlfriends, fast-food joints, hanging out at the mall and quad theaters. But computer whiz Frank and the charming, athletic Joe are deep into international intrigue and high-tech drama. The pace of these mysteries just never lets up!

For a sample of the *new* Hardy Boys, turn the page and enjoy an excerpt from DEAD ON TARGET and EVIL, INC., the first two books in THE HARDY BOYS CASEFILES.

And don't forget to look for more of the new Hardy Boys and details about a great Hardy Boys contest in April!

THE HARDY BOYS CASEFILES™

Case #1
Dead on Target

A terrorist bombing sends Frank and Joe on a mission of revenge.

"GET OUT OF *my way, Frank!*" Joe Hardy shoved past his brother, shouting to be heard over the roar of the flames. Straight ahead, a huge fireball rose like a mushroom cloud over the parking lot. Flames shot fifty feet into the air, dropping chunks of wreckage—wreckage that just a moment earlier had been their yellow sedan. "Iola's in there! We've got to get her out!"

Frank stared, his lean face frozen in shock, as his younger brother ran straight for the billowing flames. Then he raced after Joe, catching him in a flying tackle twenty feet away from the blaze. Even at that distance they could feel the heat.

"Do you want to get yourself killed?" Frank yelled, rising to his knees.

Joe remained silent, his blue eyes staring at the wall of flame, his blond hair mussed by the fall.

Frank hauled his brother around, making Joe face him. "She wouldn't have lasted a second," he said, trying to soften the blow. "Face it, Joe."

For an instant, Frank thought the message had gotten through. Joe sagged against the concrete. Then he surged up again, eyes wild. "No! I can save her! Let go!"

Before Joe could get to his feet, Frank tackled him again, sending both of them tumbling along the ground. Joe began struggling, thrashing against his brother's grip. With near-maniacal strength, he broke Frank's hold, then started throwing wild punches at his brother, almost as if he were grateful to have a physical enemy to attack.

Frank blocked the flailing blows, lunging forward to grab Joe again. But a fist pounded through his guard, catching him full in the mouth. Frank flopped on his back, stunned, as his brother lurched to his feet and staggered toward the inferno.

Painfully pulling himself up, Frank wiped something wet from his lips—blood. He sprinted after Joe, blindly snatching at his T-shirt. The fabric tore loose in his hand.

Forcing himself farther into the glare and suffocating heat, Frank managed to get a grip on his brother's arm. Joe didn't even try to shake free. He just pulled both of them closer to the flames.

The air was so hot it scorched Frank's throat as he gasped for breath. He flipped Joe free, throwing him off balance. Then he wrapped one arm around Joe's neck and cocked the other back, flashing in a karate blow. Joe went limp in his brother's arms.

As Frank dragged them both out of danger, he heard the wail of sirens in the distance. We should never have come, he thought, never.

Just an hour before, Joe had jammed the brakes on the car, stopping in front of the mall. "So *this* is why we had to come here," he exclaimed. "They're having a rally! Give me a break, Iola."

"You knew we were working on the campaign." Iola grinned, looking like a little dark-haired pixie. "Would you have come if we'd told you?"

"No way! What do you think, we're going to stand around handing out Walker for President buttons?" Joe scowled at his girlfriend.

"Actually, they're leaflets," Callie Shaw said from the backseat. She leaned forward to peer at herself in the rearview mirror and ran her fingers hastily through her short brown hair.

"So that's what you've got stuck between us!" Frank rapped the cardboard box on the seat.

"I thought you liked Walker," said Callie.

"He's all right," Frank admitted. "He looked good on TV last night, saying we should fight back against terrorists. At least he's not a wimp."

"That antiterrorism thing has gotten a lot of coverage," Iola said. "Besides . . ."

". . . He's cute," Frank cut in, mimicking Iola.

"The most gorgeous politician I've ever seen."

Laughter cleared the air as they pulled into a parking space. "Look, we're not really into passing out pamphlets—or leaflets, or whatever they are," Frank said. "But we will do something to help. We'll beef up your crowd."

"Yeah," Joe grumbled. "It sounds like a real hot afternoon."

The mall was a favorite hangout for Bayport kids—three floors with more than a hundred stores arranged around a huge central well. The Saturday sunshine streamed down from the glass roof to ground level—the Food Floor. But that day, instead of the usual tables for pizzas, burgers, and burritos, the space had been cleared out, except for a band, which was tuning up noisily.

The music blasted up to the roof, echoing in the huge open space. Heads began appearing, staring down, along the safety railings that lined the shopping levels. Still more shoppers gathered on the Food Floor. Callie, Iola, and four other kids circulated through the crowd, handing out leaflets.

The Food Floor was packed with people cheering and applauding. But Frank Hardy backed away, turned off by all the hype. Since he'd lost Joe after about five seconds in the jostling mob, he fought his way to the edges of the crowd, trying to spot him.

Joe was leaning against one of the many pillars supporting the mall. He had a big grin on his face and was talking with a gorgeous blond girl. Frank hurried over to them. But Joe, deep in conversation with his new friend, didn't notice his brother. More importantly, he didn't notice his girlfriend making her way through the crowd.

Frank arrived about two steps behind Iola, who had wrapped one arm around Joe's waist while glaring at the blond. "Oh, uh, hi," said Joe, his grin fading in embarrassment. "This is Val. She just came—"

"I'd love to stay and talk," Iola said, cutting Joe off, "but we have a problem. We're running out of leaflets. The only ones left are on the backseat of your car. Could you help me get them?"

"Right now? We just got here," Joe complained.

"Yeah, and I can see you're really busy," Iola said, looking at Val. "Are you coming?"

Joe hesitated for a moment, looking from Iola to the blond girl. "Okay." His hand fished around in his pocket and came out with his car keys. "I'll be with you in a minute, okay?" He started playing catch with the keys, tossing them in the air as he turned back to Val.

But Iola angrily snatched the keys in midair. Then she rushed off, nearly knocking Frank over.

"Hey, Joe, I've got to talk to you," Frank said, smiling at Val as he took his brother by the elbow. "Excuse us a second." He pulled Joe around the pillar.

"What's going on?" Joe complained. "I can't even start a friendly conversation without everybody jumping on me."

"You know, it's lucky you're so good at picking up girls," said Frank. "Because you sure are tough on the ones you already know."

Joe's face went red. "What are you talking about?"

"You know what I'm talking about. I saw your little trick with the keys there a minute ago. You made Iola look like a real jerk in front of some girl you've been hitting on. Make up your mind, Joe. Is Iola your girlfriend or not?"

Joe seemed to be studying the toes of his running shoes as Frank spoke. "You're right, I guess," he finally muttered. "But I was gonna go! Why did she have to make such a life-and-death deal out of it?"

Frank grinned. "It's your fatal charm, Joe. It stirs up women's passions."

"Very funny." Joe sighed. "So what should I do?"

"Let's go out to the car and give Iola a hand," Frank suggested. "She can't handle that big box all by herself."

He put his head around the pillar and smiled at Val. "Sorry. I have to borrow this guy for a while. We'll be back in a few minutes."

They headed for the nearest exit. The sleek, modern mall decor gave way to painted cinderblocks as they headed down the corridor to the underground parking garages. "We should've caught up to her by now," Joe said as they came to the first row of cars. "She must be really steamed."

He was glancing around for Iola, but the underground lot was a perfect place for hide-and-seek. Every ten feet or so, squat concrete pillars which supported the upper levels rose from the floor, blocking the view. But as the Hardys reached the end of the row of cars, they saw a dark-haired figure marching angrily ahead of them.

"Iola!" Joe called.

Instead of turning around, Iola put on speed.

"Hey, Iola, wait a minute!" Joe picked up his pace, but Iola darted around a pillar. A second later she'd disappeared.

"Calm down," Frank said. "She'll be outside at the car. You can talk to her then."

Joe led the way to the outdoor parking lot, nervously pacing ahead of Frank. "She's really angry," he said as they stepped outside. "I just hope she doesn't—"

The explosion drowned out whatever he was going to say. They ran to the spot where they'd parked their yellow sedan. But the car—and Iola—had erupted in a ball of white-hot flame!

Case #2
Evil, Inc.

When Frank and Joe take on Reynard and Company, they find that murder is business as usual.

THE FRENCH POLICE officer kept his eyes on the two teenagers from the moment they sat down at the outdoor café across the street from the Pompidou Center in Paris.

Those two kids spelled trouble. The cop knew their type. *Les punks* was what the French called them. Both of them had spiky hair; one had dyed his jet black, the other bright green. They wore identical black T-shirts emblazoned with the words *The Poison Pens* in brilliant yellow, doubtless some unpleasant rock group. Their battered, skintight black trousers seemed ready to split at the seams. And their scuffed black leather combat boots looked as if they had gone through a couple of wars. A gold earring gleamed on one earlobe of each boy.

What were they waiting for? the cop wondered. Somebody to mug? Somebody to sell drugs to? He was sure of one thing: the punks were up to no good as they sat waiting and watchful at their table, nursing tiny cups of black coffee. True, one of them looked very interested in any pretty girl who passed by. But when a couple of girls stopped in front of the table, willing to be friendly, the second punk said something sharp to the first, who shrugged a silent apology to the girls. The girls shrugged back and went on their way, leaving the two punks to scan the passing crowd.

The cop wished he could hear their conversation and find out what language they spoke. You couldn't tell kids' nationalities nowadays by their appearance. Teen styles crossed all boundaries, he had decided.

If the cop had been able to hear the two boys, he would have known instantly where they were from.

"Cool it. This is no time to play Casanova," one of them said.

"Aw, come on," the other answered. "So many girls—so little time."

Their voices were as American as apple pie, even if their appearances weren't.

In fact, their voices were the only things about them that even their closest friends back home would have recognized.

"Let's keep our minds on the job," Frank Hardy told his brother.

"Remember what they say about all work and no play," Joe Hardy answered.

"And *you* remember that if we make one wrong move here in Paris," Frank said, "it'll be our last."

Sitting in the summer late-afternoon sunlight at the Café des Nations, Frank was having a hard time keeping Joe's mind on business. He had no sooner made Joe break off a budding friendship with two pretty girls who had stopped in front of their table, when another one appeared. One look at her, and Frank knew that Joe would be hard to discourage.

She looked about eighteen years old. Her pale complexion was flawless and untouched by makeup except for dark shading around her green eyes. Her hair was flaming red, and if it was dyed, it was very well done. She wore a white T-shirt that showed off her slim figure, faded blue jeans that hugged her legs down to her bare ankles, and high-heeled sandals. Joe didn't have to utter a word to say what he thought of her. His eyes said it all: Gorgeous!

Even Frank wasn't exactly eager to get rid of her.

Especially when she leaned toward them, gave them a smile, and said, "Brother, can you spare a million?"

"Sit down," Joe said instantly.

But the girl remained standing. Her gaze flicked toward the policeman who stood watching them.

"Too hot out here in the sun," she said with the faintest of French accents. "I know someplace that's cooler. Come on."

Frank left some change on the table to pay for the coffees, then he and Joe hurried off with the girl.

"What's your name?" Joe asked.

"Denise," she replied. "And which brother are you, Joe or Frank?"

"I'm Joe," Joe said. "The handsome, charming one."

"Where are we going?" asked Frank.

"And that's Frank," Joe added. "The dull, businesslike one."

"Speaking of business," said Denise, "do you have the money?"

"Do you have the goods?" asked Frank.

"*Trust* the young lady," Joe said, putting his arm around her shoulder. "Anyone who looks as good as she does can't be bad."

"First, you answer," Denise said to Frank.

"I've got the money," said Frank.

"Then I've got the goods," said Denise.

The Hardys and Denise were walking through a maze of twisting streets behind the Pompidou Center. Denise glanced over her shoulder each time they turned, making sure they weren't being followed. Finally she seemed satisfied.

"In here," she said, indicating the entranceway to a grime-covered old building.

They entered a dark hallway, and Denise flicked a switch.

"We have to hurry up the stairs," she said. "The light stays on for just sixty seconds."

At the top of the creaking stairs was a steel door, which clearly had been installed to discourage thieves. Denise rapped loudly on it: four raps, a pause, and then two more.

The Hardys heard the sound of a bolt being unfastened and then a voice saying, *"Entrez."*

Denise swung the door open and motioned for Frank and Joe to go in first.

They did.

A man was waiting for them in the center of a shabbily furnished room.

Neither Frank nor Joe could have said what he looked like.

All they could see was what was in his hand.

It was a pistol—and it was pointed directly at them.

And don't miss these other exciting all-new adventures in THE HARDY BOYS CASEFILES

Case #3
Cult of Crime

High in the untamed Adirondack Mountains lurks one of the most fiendish plots Frank and Joe Hardy have ever encountered On a mission to rescue their good friend Holly from the cult of the lunatic Rajah, the boys unwittingly become the main event in one of the madman's deadly rituals—human sacrifice.

Fleeing from gun-wielding "religious" zealots and riding a danger-infested train through the wilderness, Frank and Joe arrive home to find the worst has happened. The Rajah and his followers have invaded Bayport. As their hometown is about to go up in flames, the boys look to Holly for help. But Holly has plans of her own, and one deadly secret.

Available in May 1987.

Case #4
The Lazarus Plot

Camped out in the Maine woods, the Hardy boys get a real jolt when they glimpse Joe's old girlfriend, Iola Morton. Can it really be the same girl who was blown to bits before their eyes by a terrorist bomb? Frantically searching for her, Frank and Joe are trapped in the lair of the most diabolical team of scientists ever assembled.

Twisting technology to their own ends, the criminals create perfect replicas of the boys. Now the survival of a top-secret government intelligence organization is at stake. Frank and Joe must discover the bizarre truth about Iola and face their doubles alone—before the scientists unleash one final, deadly experiment.

Available in June 1987.

MEET THE

DREAM GIRLS™

The exciting new soap-opera series

DREAM GIRLS™ is the enchanting new series that has all the glamour of the Miss America Pageant, the intrigue of Sweet Valley High, and the chance to share the dreams and schemes of girls competing in beauty pageants.

In DREAM GIRLS™ you will meet Linda Ellis, a shy, straightforward beautiful girl entering the fast-paced world of beauty contests. Vying for the limelight with Linda is Arleen McVie who is as aggressive, devious and scheming as she is attractive. Join Linda and Arleen as they compete for the scholarships, the new wardrobes, the prizes, the boyfriends and the glitz of being number one!

Come share the dream as you join the DREAM GIRLS™ backstage in their quest for fame and glory.

#1 ANYTHING TO WIN
#2 LOVE OR GLORY?
#3 TARNISHED VICTORY
#4 BOND OF LOVE
#5 TOO CLOSE FOR COMFORT
#6 UP TO NO GOOD

Archway Paperbacks
Published by Pocket Books,
A Division of Simon & Schuster, Inc.